KT-495-919

The Unicorns of Blossom Wood

Scholastic Children's Books
An imprint of Scholastic Ltd
Euston House, 24 Eversholt Street, London, NW1 1DB, UK
Registered office: Westfield Road, Southam, Warwickshire, CV47 0RA
SCHOLASTIC and associated logos are trademarks and/or
registered trademarks of Scholastic Inc.

First published in the UK by Scholastic Ltd, 2017

Text copyright © Catherine Coe, 2017
Cover copyright © Andrew Farley represented by Meiklejohn, 2017
Inside illustration copyright © Renée Kurilla, 2017

The right of Catherine Coe and Renée Kurilla to be identified as the
author and illustrator of this work has been asserted by them.

ISBN 978 1407 17125 8

A CIP catalogue record for this book
is available from the British Library.

All rights reserved.
This book is sold subject to the condition that it shall not,
by way of trade or otherwise, be lent, hired out or otherwise circulated in
any form of binding or cover other than that in which it is published. No
part of this publication may be reproduced, stored in a retrieval system,
or transmitted in any form or by any means (electronic, mechanical,
photocopying, recording or otherwise) without prior
written permission of Scholastic Limited.

Printed by CPI Group (UK) Ltd, Croydon, CR0 4YY

Papers used by Scholastic Children's Books are made
from wood grown in sustainable forests.

9 10

This is a work of fiction. Names, characters, places, incidents
and dialogues are products of the author's imagination or are used
fictitiously. Any resemblance to actual people, living or dead,
events or locales is entirely coincidental.

www.scholastic.co.uk

Catherine Coe

Unicorn games & quizzes inside!

The Unicorns of Blossom Wood

Best Friends

SCHOLASTIC

For Wolfram and Janka – meine wunderbaren
deutschen Eltern xxx

Thanks to Dina von Lowenkraft for all your
invaluable advice and suggestions.

Chapter 1
A Last Adventure

"I can't believe it's the last day of our holiday," said Lei, her brown eyes filling up with tears as she dived into the tent. "And then I won't get to see you both until next summer!"

Squeezing in after her, Cora nodded, and put an arm around her American cousin. "It sucks!"

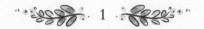

"But we can still call and video chat," Isabelle reminded them. She was already in the tent, scribbling away in her diary. "We'll have to, because I won't be able to talk about Blossom Wood with anyone else, and there's no way I'll be able to keep it in!"

 2

The three cousins always had a fantastic time on holiday together, but this year it'd been even more magical. On their first day at the Hilltop Hideaway campsite they'd found hoof prints in a nearby cove. When they'd stepped in them they'd been transported to an amazing forest called Blossom Wood. What's more, when they were there, the girls were no longer girls – they were unicorns!

"That's true," said Lei with a smile. "I know it's not easy to talk to each other when we're all back home, but we'll have to find a way!" Lei lived in San Francisco, Cora in Australia and Isabelle in England, so finding a time of day when they were all awake was tricky. It was much easier when they were on holiday, and all in the same place at once!

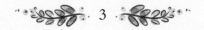

"Girls, where are you?" Cora's mum's voice floated through the tent. "It's our last night. Come and join us!"

Cora's face fell. "Oh no," she whispered. "We won't get a chance to go to the cove now!"

"Maybe we could sneak away before anyone sees us?" suggested Isabelle. "Time doesn't pass while we're in Blossom Wood, remember, so we'd only be gone for the time it takes to get down to the cove and back..."

Lei stuck her face out of the tent, then turned back to her cousins. She shook her head, revealing the pink braids beneath her long dark brown hair. "Everyone's outside. Even my sister!"

"Come on, girls, what are you doing in that tent?" asked Lei's mum.

"Um ... just, um ... talking – I'll be

 4

out in a sec," Lei told her, then whispered
back to Isabelle and Cora, "We'll just have
to try to sneak away later!" She wriggled
out of the tent, pulled on her pink pumps
and wandered over to their parents.
Isabelle and Cora quickly followed.

Everyone sat in camp chairs in a circle,
chatting, apart from Lei's older sister, Ying.
She was in a camp chair, but she had her
headphones on and her eyes shut as usual,
nodding her pink hair to her music.

"What's happening?" asked Isabelle as
she adjusted the owl hair clip in her red
curly hair.

Her mum turned around and grinned.
"We're having a campfire!" She held up
a packet of marshmallows. "I know we've
already had dessert, but it wouldn't be
a proper campfire without toasting some
of these!"

"We might have to eat them untoasted
if I can't get the fire to start," Cora's dad
groaned. He got up and bent down to
the firepit, poking it with a pair barbecue
tongs.

"What's wrong, Dad?" Cora asked,
wrapping her thick cardigan around her.
The sun was going down, turning the sky

a beautiful pinky-purple colour, and it was getting chilly on the hilltop campsite.

He sighed and stared at the pile of logs. "It just won't light properly. I think we need more kindling."

"We can help with that!" Lei shouted, a bit too loudly.

All their parents turned to look at her. "Wow, you're keen," said Lei's dad. "Do you know where to find some?"

Lei nodded like a woodpecker and grabbed Isabelle's and Cora's hands. "Yes, we do, don't we? Down near the trees by the lake, right?"

"Oh, yes," said Cora, quickly understanding Lei's plan. "There are loads of twigs and things down there."

Isabelle looked around and spotted an empty picnic hamper. "We'll be able to collect loads in this!" she said, sweeping

up the hamper and waving it around.

"All right, girls." Isabelle's mum smiled, her green eyes crinkling in the corners.

"Just don't be long – it'll be dark soon," Cora's mum said.

Cora nodded and tucked her bobbed blonde hair behind her ears. "No worries. We'll be back in a few minutes!"

The three cousins spun around, linked arms and began running down the hill towards the lake, the picnic hamper swinging like a giant bracelet on Isabelle's wrist.

"Thank chestnuts for that!" said Lei. It was something she'd heard their animal friends saying, and she liked it a lot. "We'll be able to go to Blossom Wood one last time after all!"

Cora's whole body tingled at the

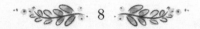

thought of seeing their woodland friends, and the beautiful forest. She wondered what would be happening there today, and what time of year it would be. Even though it was summer in their world, the seasons were often different in Blossom Wood. Last time they were there it was

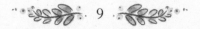

super-hot, but the time before that it had been midwinter!

Isabelle bit her lip. "I can't believe it's going to be our last time there. I feel like we're only just getting to know everyone!"

Suddenly, Cora's tingles were gone at the thought of this being their last visit to Blossom Wood. At the start of their holiday, she hadn't even believed in magic. But now she never wanted it to end! She felt hot tears swimming to her eyes, and blinked them away furiously.

The girls reached the shore of the lake, and began skipping across the sand. The small lake was still and calm, the indigo-blue water reflecting the trees and hills around it.

It reminded Lei of their first time in Blossom Wood, when they'd looked at themselves in a puddle of water and saw that they were unicorns. She wished she could go back in time and live all of their adventures again.

Isabelle noticed her cousins' downturned mouths and squeezed both of their hands. "Hey, don't be sad. We've got to enjoy this! And who knows, maybe we will be able to come back again one day."

Cora smiled at her optimistic cousin, hoping she was right, and decided to take her advice. She had to enjoy this – especially if it was their last visit.

They reached the cove, which was like a shallow cave set into the hillside. At the back, the hoof prints were waiting for them. Still holding hands, Cora, Isabelle and Lei each stepped into a set, and Isabelle set down the hamper.

Immediately, their feet fizzed with warm magic, which began spreading up their legs and through their bodies. Bright white light flashed all around them, forcing them to shut their eyes.

"Blossom Wood, here we come!" yelled Lei.

Chapter 2

Bobby the Magician

Isabelle's whole body fizzed and tingled and fizzed some more. She still had her eyes tight shut, but the bright light was disappearing now. She slowly opened them ... and gasped at the view. Even though this was her fourth time in Blossom Wood, its beauty still took her breath away. She looked down on trees in every shade of green, the leaves twinkling in the sunlight. Perfect fluffy white clouds dotted the turquoise-blue sky, and Willow Lake shone like a jewel in the distance. As usual, they'd arrived high up on a mountain, and could see the whole stunning wood stretched out beneath them.

Isabelle turned to her cousins and neighed excitedly. They were no longer girls, but unicorns again! The sight of their glossy white coats and shiny manes made Isabelle toss her own red mane in delight.

Cora blinked her blue eyes, as if she couldn't quite believe it. "We're back!" She trotted carefully out of the hoof prints that would take them home again when they were ready. As she neared the edge of the mountain, she smiled at the

powerful feeling in her unicorn legs. Cora was the biggest of the three – the size of a racehorse. She could gallop so fast everything she passed became a blur. "It looks really busy down there today..."

Lei squinted at the thick forests below. "Yeah, that's true," she said, noticing rabbits scampering and bees buzzing and birds fluttering all around. Willow Lake was filled with waves and splashes, and Foxglove Glade was crowded with creatures. "I wonder what's going on?"

Isabelle was already cantering down the rocky mountain path. "Let's go and see!" she said and whinnied, flicking her red tail as she raced along. Sparks flew from her hooves as they hit the ground – these were magical sparks, which gave Isabelle a special power. She could light up like a lantern in the dark!

Lei quickly followed her cousin, pink sparks fizzing from her own hooves to match her pink mane and tail. She'd only recently discovered her magical power – she could control the weather. But she didn't need to do anything about it today. The sunshine was warm but not too hot, and there was a gentle, refreshing breeze in the air. Lei galloped to catch up to Isabelle. She was the smallest of the unicorns, like a pony, which meant she had to work hard to move at the same speed as her cousins. Not that she minded – galloping as a unicorn was even better than riding her horse at home!

Behind them, Cora raced along. Her sparks were golden, and her magical power was healing, although she hoped she wouldn't have to use it today. Cora's

long, strong legs meant she quickly
caught up to Isabelle and Lei, and by
the time they reached the bottom of
the mountain, the three unicorns were
trotting alongside each other. They
waved to a group of little bluebirds, who

were darting about in the sky as if they were dancing. Then they passed a trio of frogs, leaping around the waterfall pool below Badger Falls.

"Look!" said Cora, spotting more than a dozen light-pink butterflies dancing like ballerinas in the air above them.

Isabelle stopped and tilted her head back. "They're so pretty."

Lei nodded, coming to a halt too. "Everyone seems full of energy today!"

"There's a good reason for that," came a deep, gravelly voice nearby.

The three unicorns looked around. The familiar figure of a badger stood beside an oak tree. "Bobby!" the cousins neighed in unison.

Bobby grinned. "It's most lovely to see you again, unicorns," he said. "You've arrived at just the right time – Loulou's organizing a talent show! She used to do one every year, but this is the first one we've had for a while. I hope you'll come to watch it? Maybe you could even join in!"

Isabelle, Cora and Lei looked at each other, their eyes wide.

"That sounds like fun," said Cora, turning to her cousins. "But what would we do?"

"Um, I'm sure we can think of something!" Lei kicked up her front hooves. "Dancing, maybe?"

Isabelle bent her head down to the badger. "What are YOU doing for it, Bobby?"

In reply, the badger held out both of his paws upwards. Each held a shiny brown chestnut. "See these chestnuts?" he said. "Now watch..."

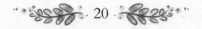

Bobby curled his paws up to hide the
nuts, then raised his arms in the air and
waved them about. "Abracadabra!" he
cried. Then he stopped waving, brought
his arms down and opened his paws
again. There was nothing inside – just
his black leathery palms.

"Ace! How did you do that?!" asked Cora.

Bobby winked. "A magician never gives away his secrets!"

"Can you do another one?" asked Lei, desperately trying to work out how Bobby had managed his trick. She knew there were some magic tricks you could do with science, like getting a straw through an apple, but where HAD those chestnuts gone?

"Well, I could – but then it would spoil the show. You'll just have to wait until tomorrow! Now, I must go and practise," he said. "If you want to find Loulou and ask to join the show, she'll most likely be up in the Moon Chestnut tree."

Bobby waved and ducked down into a tunnel, which led to his badger sett.

Isabelle turned to her cousins. "Can we be in the talent show? Please?"

Lei nodded immediately, but Cora looked worried. "I'm not sure I'm good enough at anything to be in the show," she said.

"Of course you are!" said Isabelle. "You're great at loads of stuff. But I've got a special idea for us..."

"What is it?" said Lei, flicking her pink tail impatiently. "Tell us!"

Isabelle smiled, and her green eyes shone. "A unicorn tap dance! That way we can use our sparks to make it look amazing!"

Cora made a low nickering sound. "That DOES sound amazing."

"Come on," said Lei, nodding in the direction of the Moon Chestnut tree. It was the highest tree in the wood and it was shaped just like a crescent moon, so it was easy to spot. "Let's go and ask Loulou if we can join in!"

Chapter 3

Bear Rescue

"Look at those bears," said Cora as they trotted through Pine Forest. "Are they tightrope walking?"

Lei chuckled. "I think they are. They actually look pretty good!"

Two big brown bears were tiptoeing across a rope strung high up between the trees. "Don't bounce too much!"

growled one to the other as they
wobbled across.

"It's you who's bouncing!" shouted the
other one back.

"Should we say hi?" Isabelle wondered,
staring upwards.

Cora frowned, then shook her head,
making her golden mane tumble about.
"I think we'd better leave them to it – if
we distract them they might fall off!"

They kept on along the woodland path. As they drew closer to the Moon Chestnut, all sorts of birdsong filled their ears. It came from every direction, although it wasn't exactly in harmony — some tunes were high-pitched and quick, and some were low and slow. Cora winced — it sounded like a hundred different choirs all practising at once!

"There's Loulou!" Lei galloped the last few strides to the Moon Chestnut tree and blew through her nose in greeting. Loulou was scampering down the bendy tree trunk, clutching a bunch of leaves in her mouth.

"Hi, Loulou," said Isabelle, as the squirrel reached the base of the trunk.

"Hewoo, wooniorns," Loulou replied, her mouth still full of leaves. She spat them out of her mouth for a moment.

"Hello, unicorns! I can't stop, I'm
afraid – I've got to get these leaves to
the frogs in Willow Lake, then I've got
to sort out a problem with the bunnies'
equipment ... and then the deer wanted
me for something too, I think." Loulou's

furry forehead creased in wrinkles of worry.

"Can we help you?" Cora asked.

"Yes!" Lei agreed. "We were coming to ask if we could join in with the talent show, but we can also help you out with organizing it too."

Loulou shook her head. "No. I can do it by myself! Really. I'm fine!" She wiped at her forehead with her paw.

"You don't *look* fine," said Isabelle, thinking that the normally bouncy squirrel looked extremely tired.

"Loulou!" a deep, posh voice twittered behind them. The unicorns turned to see a blackbird flying towards them with a VERY grumpy look on his face. "This is just not acceptable!"

"Charles? What's the matter?" Loulou slumped back against the tree trunk.

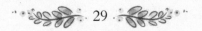

"The singing! Everyone's practising for the talent show, and I can't hear myself think. I need peace and quiet to prepare my blackbird solo!" The blackbird fanned out his tail angrily as he landed on the mossy ground.

So that's the birdsong I could hear,

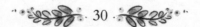

thought Cora. She wasn't surprised he was having trouble rehearsing.

"How about you fly somewhere quieter?" Isabelle asked gently. "It was nice and peaceful near Echo Mountains. Why don't you go there?"

The frown disappeared from Charles's face. "Oh, yes, well, all right then. Good idea, unicorn." With that, he gave a quick nod and fluttered back up into the sky.

"Thank you, Isabelle." Loulou sighed in relief. "The birds and their singing have been giving me trouble all day."

"See, we CAN help," said Lei. "Why don't you let us? I promise we won't get in your way."

Loulou smiled. "Um ... OK then. Thank you. Would you mind going to Willow Lake to see what the deer wanted?"

"Of course," said Cora. "And once that's done, we'll come back to see what else we can help with!"

Loulou plucked up the leaves in her mouth once more and ran off, and the cousins began cantering towards Willow Lake.

"I wonder what the deer need help with," Isabelle murmured as they raced through the wood.

As the silvery trees around Willow Lake came into sight, they heard great splashes and yelps of noise from beyond them. When they poked their heads through the curtain-like leaves, they saw five deer swimming around Willow Lake, matching each other's movements perfectly.

"I've seen this at school," Lei whispered. "It's synchronized swimming!"

"Amazing!" Cora replied.

They watched the deer all dive down at once, then spin left, then right. Then they held hooves and made a star shape in the water. However, it looked like six otters were trying to do the same thing, and everyone was getting in each other's way. Paws and hooves flew all over the place! Lei trotted to the edge of the lake, and shouted in her loudest voice, "Hey there! Can you stop a moment?"

The splashing died down and the deer and otters turned to Lei.

"The otters are taking up too much room!" complained Sara, one of the deer. "And we're trying to practise for the talent show. Where's Loulou? I asked if she could come to sort this out."

"Loulou's a bit busy," Isabelle told them. "But we've come to help instead."

"I've got an idea," said Cora, remembering what she did with her friends when they were practising dance routines in her bedroom. "Why don't you take it in turns? You'll all be very tired if you don't have a rest from time to time, and you don't want to be too tired to perform in the show."

Lei turned to the otters. "Why don't

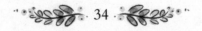

you let the deer practise first for an hour?" Then she turned to the deer and added, "And after that let the otters have a turn. You can carry on taking turns, and everyone gets to practise."

"That's a great idea!" Isabelle whispered to her cousins.

The animals in the lake were all nodding and smiling now. "We'll wait at the side of the lake while you have your turn," said one of the otters. "We can tell you if anyone's out of sync."

"That sounds perfect," said Cora with a grin. "Good luck!" she called as she and her cousins trotted away from the lake, feeling pleased they'd sorted out another problem for Loulou.

"Let's go back to the Moon Chestnut tree," Lei suggested, "and see if there's anything else we can help Loulou with."

They pushed through the willow branches once more, and began cantering back to the crescent-shaped tree. But halfway there, they heard a great growl rumbling through the forest.

"That sounds like a bear!" said Cora. She pressed her hooves down hard on the soft, earthy ground, quickening into a gallop towards the pine trees. Isabelle and Lei raced behind her, though they couldn't quite match the speed of Cora's longer legs.

Cora soon saw what was wrong. One of the bears they'd seen earlier was dangling down from the tightrope, which was now wound around his paws.

"Oh no! Are you OK?" Cora asked.

The big brown bear gave an upside-down smile. "I'm fine. Well, kind of. But I could do with some help to get down…"

The other bears stood on the ground
below him, staring up and scratching
their chins. "You're really stuck there,
Bruce," said one of them.

"I know that, Brian!" Bruce replied.
"Why aren't you helping?"

The bears continued to stare. "We don't really know what to do..." Brian replied.

"I do!" said Cora, thinking that bears didn't seem to be the cleverest of animals – although she was still impressed by how they could tightrope walk. "Can you all gather in a circle on the ground below Bruce? Then we just need to find someone who can cut the rope..."

She looked around, and spotted a bunny she recognized skipping through the trees. "Lizzie!" Cora called. "Can I ask you a favour?"

Lizzie shot over to the unicorns like an arrow. "Yes!" she squeaked. "You did rescue me from the caves, after all!" During their second visit to Blossom Wood, the unicorns had saved Lizzie when she'd got stuck in the caves below Echo Mountains.

Cora explained what she needed Lizzie to do, and soon the bunny was scampering up the pine tree, then gnawing at the rope with her long, sharp teeth.

"Ready?" Cora asked the bears as they waited beneath Bruce, their big paws outstretched.

"Ready!" they all growled in reply.

"I'm falling!" yelped Bruce as the rope broke and he dropped like a giant pine cone, but the bears beneath caught him safely in their arms. He got to his paws and beamed a right-way-up smile at Cora. "Thank you!" he said.

"No worries," Cora neighed. "Now we'd better get back to Loulou. We're helping her with the talent show."

"I wonder what she's doing in it," said Lei as they turned to go. "We forgot to ask."

"I don't think Loulou's doing anything," Brian called out as he stared up at the pine tree.

"Why not?" asked Isabelle, surprised. The talent show was Loulou's idea, after all.

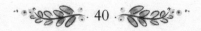

But Brian didn't reply – he was already halfway up the tree, a new rope dangling from his mouth.

"We'll have to ask Loulou," said Cora as they trotted off.

Lei nodded. "After all her hard work, she's got to perform!"

Chapter 4

The Problem with Loulou

Dusk was falling as they reached the Moon Chestnut tree, and the wood seemed much quieter now – although Isabelle thought she could still hear the odd bird singing, and even the squeaky tune of a mouse.

"Loulou!" the unicorns called up to her at the trunk of the tree. "Are you there?"

They waited a moment. Then they

heard a sniff, followed by: "Just coming!"

When Loulou poked her head out of her nest in the branches of the tree, the unicorns could see she'd been crying – her eyes were red and watery.

"What's wrong, Loulou?" asked Isabelle. "Is there a problem with the talent show?"

Loulou wrung her hands. "No, it's not that – with your help I think everything is sorted. Thank you."

"Then what's the matter?" Lei stretched her neck up high to get closer to Loulou, but she was still much further up in the tree.

The squirrel wiped her eyes with a leaf, then darted down the trunk like a spider down a drain. When she reached the bottom, she stopped and sniffed, and the unicorns sat down beside her, their eyes wide with concern.

"It's my best friend, Sophie," Loulou began in a shaky voice, dabbing another tear from her eye. "We used to do everything together – bury our nuts, run errands, swim in Willow Lake – and organize the talent show. We even had a double act – we called ourselves the Trapezing Twins."

Lei grinned. "That sounds awesome," she said, imagining two squirrels flinging themselves from branch to branch like monkeys.

"It was," said Loulou. Her face brightened with a smile for a moment, then the smile vanished. "Except ... she disappeared from Blossom Wood many, many moons ago. This is the first time I've held the talent show since she left. I thought I could do it without her. But

I just miss her so, so much!" Loulou
buried her head in her paws.

Cora's insides felt like jelly, imagining
how unhappy Loulou must be at losing
her best friend.

"Is that why you're not taking part?"
Isabelle asked gently, reaching out a hoof
to comfort her.

Loulou nodded, her face still hidden in her paws. "I can't do it without her," she said in a muffled squeak.

"I understand that," Cora neighed, wishing there was something she could do to cheer up Loulou.

"You could join in with us?" Lei stood again and pranced around in a circle. "We're going to do a dance. You could ride on my back?"

Loulou gave another smile, but it was filled with sadness. "Thanks, Lei, that's kind of you, but I think I'd just prefer to watch." She got up and shook out her tail. "Anyway, I shouldn't be here feeling sorry for myself! How did you get on with the deer?"

"All sorted," Isabelle reassured her. "And we fixed a tricky tightrope problem too."

Loulou put a paw to her head. "The bears?" All three unicorns nodded. "Dear me. They do love to tiptoe on their tightropes, but that's not the first time they've got into a muddle!"

"They were pretty funny creatures," Lei admitted. "But I liked them. And who wouldn't want to tightrope walk." It flashed through her mind whether she'd be able to try it as a unicorn, but she quickly decided that would be a very bad idea. She didn't want to break a leg or anything!

"Anyway," squeaked Loulou, "thank you from the tip of my tail for the help you've given me today. I couldn't have got everything sorted without you." She swung her bushy tail around to hide a yawn, and her eyelids drooped.

"You look so tired, Loulou," neighed

Cora. "Are you going to take a rest now?"

The squirrel smiled and nodded. "Yes, I think I'll have an early night. I want to be fresh in the morning for the talent show. See you tomorrow!"

Loulou gave them a wave, then darted up the tree trunk. Lei watched in awe. *How can she climb up it like that?* she wondered. *She must have very sharp claws!*

Meanwhile, Isabelle was thinking something else entirely. If they were going to stay for the talent show, they'd have to sleep here overnight. Which only meant one thing... "Blossom Wood sleepover!" Isabelle yelled out loud, grinning madly at her two cousins.

Lei pranced in place, sending pink sparks everywhere. "I hadn't thought of that! Cool!"

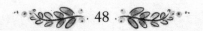

Cora looked around. "But WHERE
will we sleep? We can't go to bed in a
tree like Loulou..."

They were all quiet for a moment. Lei
thought of all their adventures around
Blossom Wood. Where would be cosy
and warm? "How about the caves,
where we rescued Lizzie?" she suggested.

"There was lots of room in there, and Isabelle can light it up for us."

Cora nodded. "That sounds like a good plan. And, actually, I'm stuffed. I could go to sleep right now!"

"Stuffed? Really?" Isabelle asked with a frown. "But our dinner at the campsite was ages ago."

Cora laughed. "Stuffed means tired in Australia!"

"Oh. I like it." Isabelle grinned. "I'm stuffed too!"

They trotted towards the caves under Echo Mountains, yawning in the moonlight. Blossom Wood was almost silent now, the only sounds the occasional rustling of a tree and the odd final bird call of the day.

When they reached the entrance to the caves, Isabelle began prancing in place,

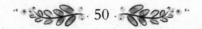

sending red sparks shooting up from the ground. Warm magic flooded into her hooves, and up her legs, body, neck and head. She was so fizzy with magic that Isabelle felt like a bottle of cola.

"Am I bright enough yet?" Isabelle

asked her cousins, sparks tingling out of her horn.

Lei laughed loudly. "If you were any brighter, I'd have to wear sunglasses," she joked.

Isabelle went into the cave first – a unicorn-shaped lantern lighting the way. Inside, Isabelle's light reflected off the multicoloured stalactites dangling from the ceiling, making them look even more magical. Stunning stalagmites also stretched up from the floor, but Isabelle spotted a clear patch of smooth rock where they could lie down to sleep.

Cora and Lei followed, settling down beside their cousin.

"Goodnight in the moonlight, see you when the sun's in sight," they chorused – it was their usual night-time rhyme, which they always sang when they were together.

"Our first ever unicorn sleepover," squealed Lei. Her body buzzed with so much excitement, she thought she'd never get to sleep. But it turned out that, like Isabelle and Cora, she was stuffed too. She'd only had her eyes shut for a few seconds before she was snoring gently, and dreaming of tightrope-walking bears.

Chapter 5
The Talent Show

When Cora opened her eyes the next morning, she had no idea where she was. She could see stalagmites and stalactites in the dimness, lit only by a few rays of sunlight that managed to make their way inside. Then she turned sideways and gasped at the sight of two unicorns beside her, remembering that she was one too!

She scrambled to her feet, sending golden sparks shooting from her hooves as they hit the ground, and soon Isabelle and Lei were stirring next to her. Moments later, they were on their hooves too.

Isabelle neighed. "It's the talent show today!"

"We'd better get practising our dance!" said Lei, prancing in place.

Nerves needled inside Cora like worms – they'd been so busy helping Loulou yesterday, they hadn't had any time at all to rehearse their performance.

"Oh, look!" Lei had spotted something near the entrance to the cave. It was a picnic hamper with a note on top:

Dear unicorns,
  Thank you for all your help yesterday.
  I thought you might like a Blossom

Wood breakfast when you woke up. I hope you enjoy it.

See you in Foxglove Glade at noon for the show!

Loulou xxx

"Loulou must have overheard us talking about our sleepover!" said Isabelle. "She's so thoughtful."

Lei pushed her nose against the hamper. It smelled of sweet pastries and home-baked bread and fresh fruit. Sure enough, when she tugged off the cloth cover, that was exactly what was inside.

"Yummy! Let's eat these fast, and then we can practise our dance!"

By the end of the morning, the cousins felt ready for the talent show. Inside the cave, with Isabelle using her light magic, they'd rehearsed their tap dance at least a hundred times.

"I can't wait to see the other performances," said Isabelle, as they stepped out of the cave and began trotting towards Foxglove Glade. They joined a throng of other woodland creatures, all heading to the glade too, and chattering excitedly about the show and the acts they were most looking forward to seeing.

The unicorns had never seen the glade so full of animals before – and so pretty too. The foxglove flowers that surrounded

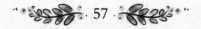

it were lit up by fireflies buzzing above, and shimmery silvery bunting had been strung around the trees.

The unicorns found a place to sit near the back of the glade, beside Bobby. "Are you ready for your first ever Blossom

Wood talent show?" he asked, clapping his paws together.

"Oh, YES!" the unicorns replied in unison.

Lei pointed her horn at the stage, which was a sloped patch of grass at the other end of the glade. "There's Loulou!"

The squirrel darted into the middle of the stage, and opened her arms to the crowd of animals, birds and insects gathered there. Everyone stopped their chatter and turned to face Loulou.

"Welcome, woodlanders, to the Blossom Wood Talent Show!" she squeaked. "I know it's been a while since the last one, but I hope that means that this show will be even more magical, even if we don't have everybody here..." Loulou pulled a leaf from her pocket and dabbed at her eyes.

"Poor Loulou," Cora whispered.

"She's being so brave," Isabelle replied.

Loulou sniffed before continuing, "As usual, the performances will happen in different places, starting here in Foxglove Glade, so we'll be moving around during the show. Now, are you ready?"

Foxglove Glade erupted in shouts and cheers. "Yes!" everyone yelled.

"Then the talent show will begin! First to the stage are our very special duck band, the Quackers..."

Loulou scampered away as a group of mallard ducks got to the stage – a mixture of brown females and green-and-purple males. The unicorns recognized the band from the midwinter festival, when they'd played some toe-tapping wintry songs. With a male drake conducting at the front, they were soon playing quick melodies that had everyone swaying and clapping to the music.

The duck band was followed by the Honeybee Waggle – a funny buzzing dance performed by what seemed to be a thousand bees in the sky above the glade.

"It really does look like a waggle!" said Lei as their little bee behinds swung back and forth.

Next came a family of bunnies who the unicorns recognized: Lizzie, Billy and Ruby. "What are they going to do

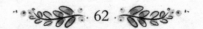

with those?" Isabelle wondered, looking at the large rings they were holding.

Her question was soon answered when they each slipped a ring over their head and began twisting their hips to keep it up. They were hula-hooping! They even waved their hands in the air, kicked out their legs and twitched their tails as the rings spun around.

"They can hula-hoop much better than I can!" said Cora with a neigh.

Then came Charles the blackbird, who sang a high, classical tune, with lots of trills and tweets, followed by two mice, named Mo and May, who sang a love song called "Cheese for Two".

Lei turned to Isabelle, Cora and Bobby. "Those mice are so cute!"

Next Loulou introduced a wren family, who did a song-and-dance routine in the sky, and then came the butterflies the unicorns had seen practising the day before, who performed a daring sky-flying routine, with spins and loop the loops.

As the last of the butterflies flew off, Wilf and three other caterpillars slithered on. They did a juggling act with hundreds of acorns, bouncing them from their many feet up in the air to each other.

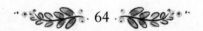

"They're much better than any clown I've ever watched!" said Isabelle.

Then, when a beaver called Jonny came onstage and began to breakdance, the unicorns couldn't stop giggling. He spun and danced and even stood on his head. Cora gasped. "I've never seen a beaver doing a backflip before!"

As Jonny's dance came to an end, Bobby pushed himself up. "It's me next!" he said, lumbering over to the stage.

Everyone loved Bobby's magic tricks – from his disappearing chestnuts to even pulling a rabbit out of a hat. When he finished, Loulou asked the woodlanders to turn to the trees – where the bears were ready and waiting to perform their tightrope walking.

It was quite a sight – big, heavy bears prancing across a thin rope – but they did it beautifully, without a single bounce! "I'm glad we don't have to untie one of them again," whispered Isabelle.

Next, Loulou ushered the audience to the shore of Willow Lake, where they watched first the deer doing their

synchronized swimming, then the otters. This was followed by three frogs performing a gymnastics routine across the lily pads. Lei gazed at them in wonder. "I wish I could jump as high as they can!"

As the frogs leapt out of the lake,

Loulou clapped her paws together. "It's time for our last act now — performed by three special creatures who helped me so much yesterday. It's the Blossom Wood unicorns: Isabelle, Lei and Cora. Unicorns, I have something special planned for you!"

Waving an arm with a flourish, Loulou turned to the lake, and everyone looked to see what she meant.

"Are the lily pads moving?" asked Cora, her blue eyes growing wider than ever before.

"It's a special Blossom Wood dance floor!" Bobby explained, pointing at the lily pads that were knitting together like a blanket across the water. When the unicorns looked unsure, he added, "It's much stronger than it looks. It'll hold you, I promise!"

Cora, Isabelle and Lei trotted to the edge of the lake. Lei was the first to step on the lily pads, placing a hoof as if she was stepping on to delicate glass. But once she felt how strong it was, she quickly trotted on to it with the rest of her hooves, and Isabelle and Cora copied her.

They took their positions, standing in a line, horns bent down low, and Cora counted them in: "One, two, three, four..."

The unicorns raised their heads and began to tap dance. First with their forelegs, then with the back legs – then with all their legs together! Red, pink and gold sparks flew as their hooves hit the lily pads, making their dancing look even more magical. They swished their manes and their tails, then trotted around in a conga style, first one way, then the other. They spun and they leapt and they kicked and they flicked, surrounded by their unicorn sparkles and enjoying every second.

As their dance came to the end, Isabelle began prancing in place, her light magic building around her so she lit up like one big unicorn firework. She raised her head to the sky, and Cora and Isabelle did the same, touching the tips of their horns and sending sparks shooting upwards.

Even more magic seemed to whip around them then, without the unicorns even needing to stamp their hooves – the sparks like a swarm of fireflies. All three of them felt tingly and warm – as if something extra magical was happening, although they had no idea what.

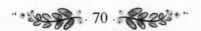

The audience of woodlanders hooted and cheered and clapped and waved as the magic continued to spin around them like a glittering tornado, their horns still touching in the air. Eventually it died away, and the unicorns stepped away from each other and gave a bow.

As they did so, the crowd gasped when they saw what was standing between the unicorns...

Chapter 6

The Most Magical Surprise

"Sophie? SOPHIE!" Loulou came scampering on to the lily-pad dance floor.

A little squirrel stood below the unicorns, blinking her eyes as if she couldn't believe what she was seeing. "What... Where am I?" she squeaked, in a voice so quiet only

Cora, Lei and Isabelle could hear her.

"You're in Blossom Wood," Cora said gently, still feeling tingly from all the incredible magic of moments before.

"Really?" The squirrel's eyes grew as large as acorns as Loulou dashed up and wrapped her arms around Sophie tightly.

"Sophie! I never thought I'd see you again!" Big tears dripped down Loulou's nose, but the unicorns were pretty sure they were tears of happiness this time. "Where have you been?"

"I got lost, searching for cedar nuts – do you remember that day I went out looking for them?"

Loulou nodded. "I didn't know what had happened to you. I thought maybe you'd decided you needed a change from Blossom Wood."

Sophie squeaked in reply. "Oh no! I was planning to come back. But I went so far, I couldn't find my way home – I've been living in a forest many lands away, although it's never been the same as Blossom Wood." She broke away from Loulou's embrace for a moment. "What

I don't understand is, I was there just a minute ago – so how did I get back here?"

A cough came from behind them. Bobby was padding across the lily-pad floor. "I think I can guess the answer to that. Unicorn magic. And the most special kind, too!"

The three cousins turned their heads to Bobby. "What do you mean?" asked Lei.

"The magic that surrounded you was even more amazing than your usual magic – so sparkly and warm and powerful. I could feel the heat all the way over on the lake shore! I think something extra special happened when you put your horns together, you see. All of your special magic joined to create something very powerful indeed. The magic to grant a wish!"

That made sense to Cora. "I *had* been hoping that Sophie and Loulou would be reunited," she said. "Do you really think our magic brought Sophie back?"

A beam stretched across Bobby's stripy face. "I think that's the only explanation!"

The two little squirrels stared up at the unicorns. "How can I ever thank you?" asked Loulou, still hugging her best friend close.

Isabelle neighed and shook her head. "Seeing how happy you both are is enough thanks for us, isn't it?"

Lei and Cora nodded quickly. Lei couldn't remember feeling this happy about anything before – and she still couldn't quite believe it was their unicorn magic that had done it. It was the perfect way to end their last adventure here.

"I thought I'd lost Blossom Wood for ever," Sophie squeaked, her tail twitching madly with excitement. "But I never stopped thinking about it – about you, Loulou, and about all the wonderful creatures here. I've missed it so much!"

Bobby coughed again, louder this time, and turned to address the whole crowd, who were still standing on the shore of the lake. "Ahem, ahem! Woodlanders, I think this goes to show that no one can ever truly lose Blossom Wood. Once you find it, it stays in your heart for ever. Somehow, the special magic found here will always bring you back." He looked up at the unicorns then, and gave them a little wink.

Isabelle caught the eyes of Cora and Lei, and they smiled at each other. At that moment, all three of them knew that this wouldn't be their last time in Blossom Wood. They would find a way back – maybe with the help of a little unicorn magic!

"Now," Bobby continued, "I think all that's left is to thank Loulou for putting on the most incredible talent show." A roar of applause started up – clapping paws, hooves, antennae and wings – until Loulou ran up beside Bobby.

"Actually, Bobby, there is something else." The beaming squirrel turned to her long-lost best friend. "If Sophie agrees, I'd like us to perform our special talent-show act – the Trapezing Twins. If the woodlanders would like to see it?" At that, the clapping grew even louder.

"Loulou and Sophie! Loulou and Sophie! Loulou and Sophie!" the crowd began to chant.

Sophie grinned and darted over. "It's a brilliant idea!"

The squirrels took their positions in one of the willow trees beside the lake. On Loulou's count, they began swinging across the branches, joining paws to swing each other up and around, from branch to trunk to leaf and then back again. Loulou flew through the air, then Sophie, then Loulou again.

"They're trapezing!" Isabelle neighed. "I wonder if we can try THAT at home."

"Hmm, I think we might be better off leaving it to the squirrels," said Cora. "Unless you want to break something!"

When the squirrels did one last triple spinning swing right over the top of the tree, then landed like gymnasts on the ground, the woodlanders' cheers became so loud they were almost deafening.

"Thank you, everyone, for watching and performing in the talent show," Loulou squeaked, a little out of breath from her performance. "Most of all, thank you, unicorns, for not only helping and performing, but for making my biggest wish come true."

The three cousins whinnied loudly. "It was our pleasure," said Lei. "Thank you for having us here!"

"See you again soon?" asked Bobby, as all the creatures began leaving now the show was over. Many were yawning heavily – it was very late, and well past the bedtimes of the younger animals.

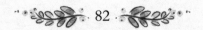

Isabelle neighed. "We hope so, Bobby, we really do." She bent her head down to the badger, nuzzling him goodbye, and Lei and Cora copied her.

"A unicorn hug!" Bobby said in his gravelly voice. "Now that's rather magical too!"

The unicorns stretched upwards again and turned towards Echo Mountains. "Goodbye, everyone!" they called as they began trotting towards the mountain path.

With her mind whirling with both happiness and sadness, Cora couldn't bear to turn back to look. But she knew that the woodlanders would all be waving goodbye – especially Bobby, Loulou and Sophie.

No one said a word on their journey through Blossom Wood. Lei, Cora and Isabelle were all lost in their own thoughts of this amazing place, and what a magical time they'd had here.

It was only when they each stepped into their sets of hoof prints on the mountainside, and magic began to tingle into their hooves, that Lei broke the silence. "Even though we're leaving each other tomorrow, this isn't our last time in Blossom Wood. I know it!" Lei looked into Isabelle's eyes, then into Cora's.

The cousins beamed, and Isabelle added, "Because nothing can separate best friends for long!"

The three best friends all neighed

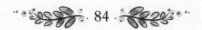

together. Dazzling light made them shut
their eyes, and magic filled their bodies,
fizzing like popping candy. They'd be
back for more magical adventures in
Blossom Wood, but for now, this one
had surely been the most magical of all.

Quiz Time

Which unicorn power do you have? Take this quiz to find out!

1 – What would you like to be when you grow up?

a) Actor

b) Scientist

c) Writer

2 – Which colour is your hair?

a) Red

b) Brown or black

c) Blonde

3 – What is your favourite word?

a) Wow

b) Awesome

c) Ace

4 – Do you prefer...

a)   Drawing

b)   Inventing things

c)   Listening to music

5 – Which type of weather is your favourite?

a)   Snow

b)   Lightning

c)   Sunshine

Mostly As: You have the same unicorn power as Isabelle! You can create light and bring brightness to any dark place. You love to use your gift when your friends are scared and need your help.

Mostly Bs: You have the same unicorn power as Lei! You can change the weather to anything you like – stormy, rainy, snowy or sunny. You love to use your gift to change people's moods and make them happy. Your honesty and loyalty makes you a very good friend.

Mostly Cs: You have the same unicorn power as Cora! You can heal anyone who's hurt. You love using your gift to take away someone's pain and cheer them up.

Word Search

Can you find the names of five things in Blossom Wood in this word search?

S	V	A	E	Q	Z	J	H	E	G
O	Z	M	O	U	N	T	A	I	N
L	B	U	S	R	L	K	P	U	Y
A	I	E	H	X	G	R	Y	B	A
K	Y	A	F	O	R	E	S	T	O
E	L	Z	V	S	E	U	X	H	G
F	V	A	I	B	J	A	K	Y	L
H	O	R	C	H	A	R	D	I	A
K	T	U	D	S	Y	O	K	U	D
S	I	X	R	E	A	I	N	M	E

❀ Glade ❀ Forest ❀ Mountain

❀ Lake ❀ Orchard

Spot the Difference

Can you spot five things that are
different in these pictures?

Meet

The Owls of Blossom Wood

in these magical books

Turn over for a sneak peek of another
Blossom Wood adventure!

The Owls of
Blossom Wood
A Magical Beginning

Catherine Coe

Chapter 1

An Amazing Discovery

Katie's long blonde hair billowed out as she spun round her bedroom. She was showing her two best friends the new ballet dance she'd learnt that week.

Eva and Alex sat on Katie's bed, clapping as Katie finished and did a curtsy. Eva's emerald-green eyes returned to her sketchpad, where she was halfway through a drawing of a rabbit eating a banana.

Alex peered over at Eva's drawing. The rabbit was so lifelike, it looked as if it might jump off the page. "You're brilliant at drawing," she said. "I wish I was that good. But ... you know rabbits don't eat bananas."

"Really? Oops." Eva turned to Katie,

who was now upside down, doing
handstands against her bedroom door.
"Can I borrow a rubber?"

Katie flung her long legs back to
the floor. "If I can find—" She stopped
mid-sentence and put her ear to the
door. "It's Alfie," she mouthed silently.

The girls froze and listened. *BANG*,

BANG, BANG went the door.

"I wish he'd just play by himself," whispered Katie. Her younger brother was always pestering them.

Alex bit her lip. "Maybe we should let him in?"

Katie groaned. "I do loads of stuff with him when you're not here. Remember what happened last time? He broke the bead necklaces Eva made for us!"

"So what should we do?" Eva adjusted the loom-band butterfly clip in her bobbed brown hair. "We can't go to mine – no one's there."

Alex lowered her eyes. "Nor mine. Sorry."

The girls lived next door to each other in a quiet countryside village. To the right of Katie's ivy-covered house stood a red-brick bungalow where Alex lived. On the left was Eva's ramshackle thatched cottage. The two girls often came over to Katie's after school, while their parents were still at work. They'd been friends for as long as they could remember.

"Well, I don't want to be stuck hiding in *here* all day." Katie put her hands on her hips.

Alex pressed her head to the door. "Wait – I think Alfie's gone."

Eva frowned in concentration. "I think I can hear the TV in the living room."

"You're right!" Katie said, her mouth stretching into a beam. "Let's sneak outside..." She twisted the doorknob silently, and tiptoed out to the landing. She could hear the loud laughter of a cartoon.

The three girls tottered over to the stairs. Katie pointed at a step in the middle. "Watch that one," she mouthed. "It creaks."

They stepped down carefully, but somehow in the middle Eva stumbled on a stair and slid to the bottom. She clamped her mouth shut, careful not to make a sound, while Alex and Katie stifled giggles at their clumsy friend. The three girls darted through the hallway, past Katie's dad at his laptop in the kitchen, and out into the garden. Yellow afternoon sunshine flooded the lawn, and the grass felt warm and springy under their bare feet.

"Can we sit in the hammocks?" Eva darted towards the cherry trees where Katie's mum had tied up hammocks. But a tug on her T-shirt jolted her back and she swung round. Katie was shaking her head and pointing at the living-room window. The hammocks were right in front of it! "Sorry," Eva whispered.

"What's that over there?" Alex's big brown eyes had turned to something lying far away at the end of the garden.

"It's an old chestnut tree that fell down ages ago," Katie explained. "Mum keeps saying she should get rid of it, but she never has."

Eva was already skipping towards the abandoned tree. "This is the perfect

place – Alfie can't see us at all from here."

Katie sprinted to catch Eva up, with Alex not far behind. Katie's garden was enormous, and they passed the washing line, rabbit hutch, rose bed and greenhouse before reaching the tree trunk. It lay amongst tangles of long grass and wild flowers – pretty poppies, bluebells, daisies and violets.

Eva plonked herself on one end of the trunk and ran her hands across the peeling bark. "I wonder how old the tree was."

"You can tell the age of a tree by the number of rings inside the trunk," said Alex, who loved wildlife and nature. She wandered through the long grasses to the end of the trunk – and gasped, "Huh?"

"What's up?" Katie ran to join Alex.

"Wow – it's hollow!" Katie began crawling into the trunk. "It's huge in here." Her voice echoed, as if she were in a cave.

As Katie's feet disappeared inside, Eva poked her head in. She started climbing in, then glanced back over her shoulder at Alex. "Come on – it'll be fun!"

Alex wasn't so sure – but at that moment she heard a loud shout from the top of the garden. Alfie! She dived into the trunk before he could see her.